What's That in Grandma's Big White Truck?

A Book on Reclaiming and Reuse

Story and Photos By Sally Kamprath

Sally Kamprath

- In this country, we produce over 540 million tons of construction and demolition waste a year. 90% of that is demolition waste. - EPA
- This story can get the conversation started with your little people about what we can save and how we can reuse.

Salvage Monkey is excited to help.

D1307969

This is Grandma.
She drives a big white truck.

One day Grandma saw a big excavator tearing down a house.

When she saw the piles of wood going into the dumpster it made her heartbroken.

Grandma thought, "Aren't there nice house parts that can be saved and used again?"

"What kind of items could be saved from the garbage when a house is torn down?"

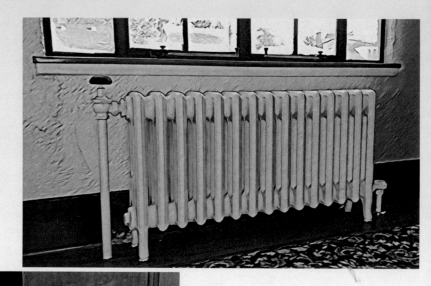

Grandma thought about her own house. It was full of doors, lights, bathtubs, floors, windows, door knobs, sinks, wood trim, cabinets, heat radiators and more.

Nate, Elliott, Jackson and little Lucas came over to visit Grandma while she was thinking about the house that was torn down.
She told the boys about it.

"If all those house parts are
thrown in the garbage, we
will fill up all our land with
trash,"
Grandma said.

Then Grandma had an idea, and said in a loud voice,
"That's NOT trash!
Let's rescue it! Let's rehouse it!"

"What's rehouse, Grandma?" asked Jackson.

"It means to take house parts out of one house and put them into another house, giving them a new place to live," Grandma explained.

Grandma found out about another house that someone wanted to tear down, and she went to talk to the owner. He agreed to let grandma save some house parts before the excavator came.

"Come on boys, let's have a look around before all the workers get here," said Grandma.

"Wow, look at these pretty windows with all the colors!" said Nate.

"I like this fireplace, where you can hang Christmas stockings," exclaimed Jackson.

"Ooooh," Little Lucas touched a shiny door knob.

"What about these railings, Grandma, can someone reuse these?" asked Elliot. "Yes boys, this house has many parts that can be re-housed. I am so happy to save them." Grand-ma said with a smile.

"Grandma, where will you take all those house parts when you save them?" asked Jackson.

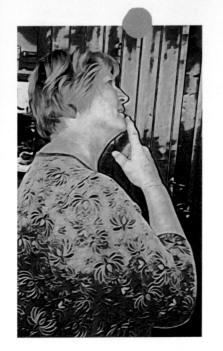

"Well, there are stores called reuse stores all over the country, and they save materials from being put in the landfill."

"We'll have a store that sells all those things, too," said Grandma as she dreamed about her new store, ... "and let's call it ReHouse!"

Nate exclaims, "And you can drive a big white truck and fill it to the top with bathtubs!"

"That's a great idea! Won't it be a sight?" says Grandma.

From a safe distance, the boys watched as Grandma and her workers started using their tools to carefully remove the house parts they wanted to save.

Grandma's big white truck was starting to fill up with a fireplace mantel, fancy leaded windows, then out came the lights and a sink.

Elliot couldn't wait to look through a box filled with shiny door knobs, heavy iron coat hooks and some old toys that were found in the attic.

Jackson jumped with glee at a bathtub with feet like a lion.

Bundles of door and window moldings were carried out of the house.

Off came the doors, the windows, a whole set of cabinets and even the kitchen sink!

The biggest pile of all was the wood wall covering.

The workers pulled all the nails from the wood and bundled it up. Now it is ready for another house to enjoy.

At the end of the day, Nate said,
"Grandma, at first it made me sad to have this house torn
down, but now it makes me happy to think we are saving so
many nice things for someone else to reuse."

Grandma gathered the boys to her and said, "Do you guys see the truck loads we're saving from the landfill?"

The boys nodded.

Well, we're a small part of a big group of hard-working people all over that are salvaging, or saving materials.

Some people also call it deconstructing. Deconstructing is taking apart and saving as many of the building materials as possible, even the biggest of boards."

"Wow," said Elliott, "We don't have *big* boards, but do you think we can make something new from the old house parts we saved?"

"I have just the thing we can make with the salvaged materials," said Grandma. "A Little Free Library! Let's get Grandpa to help!"

The boys couldn't wait to start working.

Grandpa and the boys gathered items to build a Little Free Library for Grandma's front yard. They picked out boards, a cabinet door with a window, hinges, a door latch and some trim.

Grandpa had some extra shingles for the roof in his workshop.

In no time at all, the library was all set up and full of books.

"Grandma, there's a book missing from the library," said Nate. "We need a book that tells other kids about deconstruction and reusing all the good stuff from buildings. Maybe we could write one."

"That sounds like a great idea!" Grandma exclaimed.

Little Lucas toddled over, pointing and said,

"Library! Yes!"

Time to Reclaim and Reuse Some More!

*R*eHouse Architectural Salvage was founded in 2002 in Rochester, NY, by Sally Kamprath

The mission is to salvage antique, vintage, and modern building materials that would otherwise be put in a landfill. By saving the materials they create jobs, economic growth, and an industry from something that was once considered trash.

Since 2002, they have saved over 11,000 doors alone. If laid end to end, the doors would be taller than 60 Empire State buildings, over 2.5 times taller than Mt Everest, and over 14 miles long.

Visit the ReHouse website or Facebook page for more information
www.ReHouse.com or www.facebook.com/ReHouseArchitecturalSalvage/

*F*or more information regarding deconstruction and reuse, go to the Build Reuse industry association web page at www.buildreuse.org.

Build Reuse has a vision to transform communities by creating a building industry in which used and excess materials become an asset to our communities and waste is no longer acceptable.

*F*ree Little Library is a non-profit organization that inspires a love of reading, builds community and sparks creativity by fostering neighborhood book exchanges, with over 90,000 participants world wide.

www.freelittlelibrary.org

Made in the
USA
Middletown, DE